D1323860

**To my husband and a wonderful father, David
and of course my lovely dad, Paul!**
R.R.

**For my dad,
With love,**
D.T.

First published in Great Britain 2020 by Egmont UK Limited
2 Minster Court, London EC3R 7BB
www.egmont.co.uk

Text copyright © Ruth Redford 2020
Illustration copyright © Dan Taylor 2020

Ruth Redford and Dan Taylor have asserted their moral rights.

ISBN 978 1 4052 9242 9
70084/001
Printed in Italy

A CIP catalogue record for this title is available from the British Library.

Ruth Redford   Dan Taylor

That's My DADDY!

EGMONT

When your daddy wakes up in the morning,
is he **grumpy**, **yawning** and a little bit **cross**?

Happy, **noisy**
and full of **fun**?

Does he make hot chocolate?

Or does he just **dribble**?

Does your daddy have **no hair** or **lots of hair**?

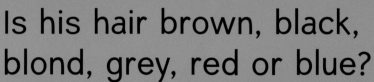
Is his hair brown, black, blond, grey, red or blue?

Does he have blue, green or brown **eyes**?

A big **nose** or a small nose?

Big **ears** or small ears? Waggly ears? Pierced ears?

Is he **tall**, **short** or **medium**?

Are his feet
GINORMOUS?
Or are they
a little bit **smelly**?!

What job does your daddy do? Is he in an office?
Does he mend the roads? Is he a **postman**?
A **builder**? A **nurse**? A **writer**? A **dancer**?

A spaceman?

Does he work . . .

in a **kitchen**?

Or outside with **animals**?

Is he a **musician**?

Or does he stay home and look after **you**?

Time's ticking on! Better get dressed.
Does your daddy wear **lots of spots** . . .

or **lots of stripes**?

Does your daddy wear a **hat** every day?

Better keep those buzzy bees away!

How does your daddy get to work?

Does he **walk slowly**?

Or drive a **fast car**?

Hop on the **bus**?

Fall asleep on the **train**?

Whizz on a **bike**?

Glide on a **scooter**?

Whoosh along on a **skateboard**?

Catch a **helicopter**?

What's your daddy like?
Is he . . .

Really **funny**?

Very **serious?**

A little bit **forgetful**?

Kind and **giving**?

Does he give the **best cuddles** in the world?

Pretend to be a **superhero**?

Let you walk on his toes?

Does your daddy do the **housework**?
There's so much to do! Does he . . .

Wash up?

Make breakfast?

Clean the bath?

Dust the chandelier!

Wash the windows? **Stack** the dishwasher?

Walk the dog?

(Or does the dog walk him?!)

Do you and your daddy **ride bikes** together?

Play outside? Kick a ball?

Or go to
the **moon**?

Paint a picture? **Play** a computer game?
Read a book? **Dance** to music until you're giddy?

Ride a unicorn?

For a special treat, what would you and Daddy do?
Go for a **swim**?

Go for a **skate**?

Visit a **park**? Visit the **zoo**?

Does your daddy **give you a bath**? Does he . . .

sing to you?

Play **peekaboo**?

Read you a story?

Sing you a song and **whisper he loves you?**

Check the cupboard for monsters?

And under the bed!

Nothing there!

Night night, Daddy!